DISNEY · PIXAR

# BRAVE

## MERIDA'S WISH

Adapted by Jasmine Jones

Cover Illustrated by Jean-Paul Orpiñas

Interior Illustrated by David Gilson

Golden® First Chapters

§ A GOLDEN BOOK • NEW YORK

randomhouse.com/kids

ISBN: 978-0-7364-2914-6 (trade)
ISBN: 978-0-7364-8107-6 (lib. bdg.)

Printed in the United States of America
10 9 8 7 6 5 4 3 2 1

My name is Merida. I'm the Princess of DunBroch, a kingdom in the Highlands of Scotland.

DunBroch is an ancient land of mist and clouds. It's a fierce, proud land, filled with stories, and magic, and danger. My story begins when the world was right. Back when everything was normal and all was fine with the kingdom.

Except it wasn't.

My father, King Fergus, was known as the Bear King because of the the gruesome way he had lost his leg to Mor'du, the evil bear. But my mother, Queen Elinor, was the real power in the kingdom—she was the lawmaker and the diplomat. And my triplet brothers, Harris, Hubert, and Hamish, were redheaded rascals disguised as princes.

Mum let those boys get away with murder. I could never get away with anything. Mum expected me to follow in her footsteps, and she was in charge of every single day of my life. "A princess is perfect!" she was always telling me. And "A princess does not chortle." And "A princess never gloats"—even when I beat my own father in a sword fight!

Mum never wanted me to eat anything tasty, do anything fun, or go anywhere interesting. It was only when I got away from her that I felt I could truly be myself. I was happiest riding my horse, Angus, in the woods, shooting arrows at targets, and doing as I pleased. But even on those days of freedom, Mum sometimes found a way to spoil things.

One day I came home from a beautiful adventure. I'd climbed the jagged rock known as the Crone's Tooth and drunk from the great waterfall called the Fire Falls. So when I returned to the castle, naturally, I was hungry. Nothing builds up an appetite like adventure.

I put a few—just a few—desserts on my plate and went to the table, where the rest of my family was already enjoying their dinner.

Well, they were enjoying it as much as they could, with Dad telling his gory story.

"Then, out of nowhere, the biggest bear

you've ever seen!" Dad was saying as I walked in. "His hide littered with the weapons of fallen warriors, his face scarred, with one dead eye! I drew me sword and—"

"*Whoosh!*" I cried, leaning close to my wide-eyed brothers. "One swipe, his sword shattered. Then *chomp!* Dad's leg was clean off! Down the monster's throat it went. Mor'du has never been seen since. And he is roaming the wilds, awaiting his chance for revenge. Argh!"

My little brothers weren't afraid. We'd all heard the story a hundred times before.

I sat down to my meal. Mum was busy reading scrolls. She didn't even look up before telling me, "A princess does not place her weapons on the table."

"Mum! It's just my bow."

She pursed her lips. "A princess should not

have weapons, in my opinion," she said.

"Leave her be," Dad said, to my relief. "Learning to fight is essential. Even for a princess."

He gave me a smile, and I felt a wee bit better. "I climbed the Crone's Tooth," I told my family, "and drank from the Fire Falls."

My father and brothers were impressed. "Fire Falls?" Dad repeated. "They say only the ancient kings were brave enough to drink the fire." He chuckled and gave me a wink. We both knew that it was only legend, but I could see that he was proud of me.

"What did you do, dear?" Mum asked, finally putting aside her scroll.

"Nothing, Mum."

That was when she noticed my food. "You'll get dreadful collywobbles," she scolded. "Fergus, will you look at your daughter's plate?"

He looked at my plate, then at his own, which was piled just as high. "So what?" he said.

Then she started in on my brothers, who hadn't touched their haggis. "Boys, how do you know you don't like it if you won't eat it?"

I took pity on my brothers. I waited until a servant came in to deliver some letters. While Mum was busy reading them, I sneaked the boys some of my sweets beneath the table.

"Fergus?" Mum said suddenly in an excited voice. "They've all accepted!"

I had a foul feeling that anything that could make my mum look so happy was sure to make me miserable. She excused my brothers, and I got the collywobbles then for sure.

"Your father has something to discuss with you," Mum announced.

Well, this was clearly news to Dad. He spit out his drink. "Merida—" he began.

Mum was too wound up to let him finish. "The clan lords are presenting their sons as suitors for your betrothal!" she gushed. "This year, each clan will present a suitor to compete for your hand in the Games."

It took a moment before I understood what she meant: nearby clans were coming to take part in the Highland Games, as they did every year. Except this year, I was going to have to marry whichever son of a numpty won! And Mum thought I'd be happy about it?

I looked to Dad for help, but he just looked at Mum.

"I suppose a princess just does what she's told!" I exclaimed.

"A princess does not raise her voice!" Mum

replied. "Merida, this is what you've been preparing for your whole life."

"No, it's what *you've* been preparing me for my whole life! I won't go through with it! You can't make me!" I shouted, and stormed away.

I heard Dad calling my name, but I didn't turn back. I ran up to my room to practice my sword fighting. I wished I could practice on those suitors.

But Mum couldn't just leave me be. She followed me.

"Suitors?" I asked as she stepped into my room. I hoped she would understand that I wasn't ready. "Marriage?"

Mum started in with one of her lectures. "Once, there was an ancient kingdom—"

I sighed. "Oh, Mum . . ."

"—its name now long forgotten, ruled by

a wise and fair king who was much beloved." Mum took the four knights from my chessboard and set them in a square on the table. "And when he grew old, he divided the kingdom among his four sons, that they should be the pillars on which the peace of the land rested." Mum picked up the chessboard—pieces and all—and set it on top of the knights. "But the oldest prince wanted to rule the land for himself. He followed his own path, and the kingdom fell. To war, and chaos, and ruin." Mum pulled one of the knights away, and the whole board fell, spilling pawns and bishops, kings and queens across the floor.

"That's a nice story," I said.

"It's not just a story, Merida," Mum told me. "Legends are lessons; they ring with truths."

I turned my back on her then. I wasn't the

least bit interested in her boring story.

"Merida! It's marriage," Mum said, annoyed. "It's not the end of the world."

I knew she thought I was being selfish, but I didn't care one bit about that. I wouldn't be married off to whichever clansman won some game. I wouldn't.

Princess or not.

Three ships arrived in our harbor the morning of the Games. At their helms were Lord Macintosh, Lord MacGuffin, and Lord Dingwall.

I watched them arrive from the window of my room. Mum had ordered her servants to stuff me into a dress and pull the laces tight. Then she shoved my wild red hair into a wimple. I felt like a stuffed sausage.

"You look absolutely beautiful," Mum said.

"I can't move," I complained. "It's too tight."

My words fell on deaf ears. "Just remember to smile," Mum told me.

How could I possibly smile? I was spending all my energy just trying to breathe!

The clansmen arrived, pouring into the Great Hall. As the lords presented their sons, I sat on my throne, wondering how to get out of being handed off to a strange suitor. And oh, what suitors!

The first was Young Macintosh. According to his father, Young Macintosh had defended our land from the Northern Invaders and vanquished *one* thousand foes with his sword. Och! He had silly hair and swished his sword around, stabbing at imaginary enemies like a fool. He had also painted himself half blue—as if that might make him seem more

courageous or brave or attractive somehow!

Next Lord MacGuffin brought his son forward. Young MacGuffin was beefy and blond, and he looked about as intelligent as my father's wooden leg. Lord MacGuffin claimed that his son had scuttled the Viking longships and vanquished *two* thousand foes. As if to prove the point, Young MacGuffin snapped a log in half with his bare hands. Charming.

Then Lord Dingwall presented his heir. "He was besieged by *ten* thousand Romans," Dingwall boasted. "And he took out a whole armada single-handedly!"

Wee Dingwall was as skinny and awkward as a baby crane. He looked like he couldn't vanquish a housefly.

As Wee Dingwall was being presented, someone from one of the other clans shouted,

"Lies!" That was all it took for fists to start flying. In a matter of seconds, our Great Hall was hosting a Great Brawl. The clans were going at it, and my father was cheering them on. He even leaped into the fray!

Finally, my mother put a stop to it.

Once order had been restored, Mum explained the rules. "In accordance with our laws, by the rights of our heritage, only the firstborn of each of the great leaders—"

I sat up. *Firstborn?*

I looked at the three dimwits before me. I had an idea.

"—may compete for the hand of the princess of DunBroch," Mum was saying. "They must prove their worth by feats of strength or arms in the Games. It is customary that the challenge be determined by the princess herself."

This was too perfect! I leaped up. "Archery!" I cried.

Mum gave me a look. I had to compose myself before I ruined everything. "I choose archery," I said as calmly as I could.

Mum nodded. "Let the Games begin!"

⁂

That afternoon on the castle grounds, men tossed cabers, threw hammers, and played tug-of-war and cricket. Bagpipes wailed and dancers twirled on tiptoe. Then it was time for the real competition.

"Archers, to your marks!" Mum declared.

Mum, Dad, and I were seated next to each other, watching. I leaned over to whisper, "Dad, ye think a-one of these gormless neeps can hit anything?"

Dad grinned at me. Then he turned to the lads and shouted, "Oi! Get on with it!"

Beefy Young MacGuffin went first. He pulled back his bowstring with a thick arm . . . and fired the arrow. It hit the target—barely.

"What a numpty," I told Dad. "I bet he wishes he was tossing cabers!"

"Or holding up bridges," Dad said with a laugh.

Next was Young Macintosh. He tossed his pretty hair and took aim.

His shot was better than Young MacGuffin's, but the arrow was still off-center. The brave lad burst into tears. He began to beat his bow against the ground.

"Oh, that's attractive," I said as he angrily threw the bow into the crowd.

Wee Dingwall was last. He reached for an

arrow and spilled everything from the quiver.

"Oh, wee lamb," I said. I felt sorry for him, I really did.

He struggled with the bow for an age. Finally, Dad shouted, "Shoot, boy!"

Startled, Wee Dingwall let go of the arrow. And would you believe it? He hit the bull's-eye.

The crowd let out a cheer. It was time.

Pulling a cloak over my head, I quickly took my bow from its hiding place beneath my throne. Then I strode over to the targets. The crowd gasped when I threw back my hood.

"I am Merida," I called, "firstborn descendant of Clan DunBroch! And I'll be shooting for my own hand!"

"What are you doing?" I heard Mum cry.

I set my arrow. But I couldn't draw back the bowstring. That dress was too tight. Taking a deep breath, I forced the seams until I felt them rip. Then I took aim and fired.

I hit the center of Young MacGuffin's target. I stepped to the next target and hit the bull's-eye that Young Macintosh had missed.

"Merida, stop this!" Mum bellowed. Out of the corner of my eye, I could see her coming toward me. "Don't you dare loose another arrow!"

But it was too late. My arrow sped forward, slicing Wee Dingwall's arrow down the center and driving halfway into the bull's-eye.

I smiled . . . for a moment. Then I came face to face with my mother.

⚜⚜

Mum dragged me off to my room for a private chat. "You embarrassed them!" she roared at me. "You don't know what you've done! It will be fire and sword if it's not set right."

"This whole marriage is what *you* want!" I yelled back. "Do you ever bother to ask me what *I* want?"

"You're acting like a child," my mother said.

"And you're a beast! That's what you are!"

I looked over at a tapestry nearby that Mum had embroidered. It was a picture of our family. I was so angry that I poked a hole in it with the tip of my sword.

Mum gasped. "Stop that!"

But I couldn't stop. "I'll never be like you. I'd rather *die* than be like you!" I cried. I slashed the tapestry, ripping it down the center, right between the images of Mum and me.

I'd never seen Mum so upset. She grabbed my sword and tossed it away. Then she took my bow—the one Dad had given me nearly ten years before—and threw it in the fire.

My beloved bow! It was in flames.

I ran from the room. There were tears streaming down my face. I had never felt this terrible in my life. I heard my mother calling my name, but I didn't look back.

Angus tore through the woods at top speed. Tears blurred my eyes. I could hardly see where we were going—and I hardly cared, just as long as we were going away from the castle.

Angus stopped suddenly, and I was thrown over his neck. I landed on the ground like a sack of beans.

When I looked up, I saw that I was in the center of a circle of tall stones as big as giants.

I had never seen the stones before. What *was* this strange place?

A blue light flickered up ahead. When I walked toward it, it whispered to me. I reached out, but it disappeared.

More blue lights suddenly appeared. They seemed to beckon me.

"Come on, Angus," I said. My horse hesitated but finally followed as I went after the blue light.

The lights led me deep into the forest to a small black hut with a low sod roof. The windows were lit, and a trickle of smoke rose from the chimney.

It turned out the place was a small woodcarver's hut. I let myself in and spotted an old woman at the back of the room. It was amazing to see what she could do with a knife and a piece of wood! And all her carvings were of bears. There were bear statues, bear charms, bears carved into the legs of tables, and more!

"Hello!" I called out to her.

"Search around to see what you like!" the woman replied. She hardly turned to greet me.

I could tell something was amiss. While the woman carved a bear statue, her broom began to sweep by itself in the corner! I wondered if the woodcarver was really a witch.

Then I spotted a crow standing atop one of the carved bears. As I moved toward the creature to take a closer look, he spoke to me!

"It's not polite to stare!" the crow said.

Now I was sure the woman was a witch. This was my chance! I asked her if she could give me just one spell.

"You see," I began, but I quickly realized

there was too much to explain, and the Witch was not particularly patient. I just wanted to tell her this was important! I wasn't ready for marriage, I could not change my mother's mind, and I certainly was in no position to change my own fate. I needed a spell!

"You'll change my fate!" I finally blurted out. "You see, it's my mother. . . ."

The woman shook her head. She refused to admit that she was a witch. She kept trying to sell me her bear carvings instead.

That gave me an idea! "I'll buy every carving you have in exchange for one spell."

She gave me an odd look. "How can you pay?" she asked.

Och, I had nothing! Then I remembered that I was still wearing a necklace Mum had given me when she had dressed me to meet the lord's sons. I quickly took it off and handed it to the Witch. It was all I had to give her.

Her eyes gleamed as she took the necklace from me and examined it. She smiled—and then pushed me out the front door!

I thought she was kicking me out, but she followed me and closed the cottage door behind us. We stood outside for just a moment before she opened the door and led us inside again. This time, things were different. Her cottage looked like a witch's cottage, and she—well, she began to act like a witch!

There was a big black cauldron in the middle of the room, and the walls were lined with bottles of potions and magical ingredients. The Witch began scurrying around, tossing a little of this and a pinch of that into the cauldron. She even plucked one of my hairs out and threw that in. Then she stirred it all with a large spoon.

"Anger made sharp," she said as she stirred, "mother's love, daughter's strife, this is the way of life." She pulled out the spoon. It had melted, so she tossed it away. She threw in something else, and white light blazed from the pot. She reached into the cauldron and pulled out . . .

"A cake?" I said with surprise. Whatever I had expected, it wasn't that.

I took the cake and she shoved me out the door. "Forget you ever saw me!" she cried.

Angus whinnied. When I turned, I saw that we were standing in the Ring of Stones. I looked back toward the Witch's cottage, and it was gone.

೩೪೩೪

I tiptoed back into the castle through the kitchen. I found a plate for the cake, then added a few extras: a cup of tea, a flower, a few berries. Did it look like a magic cake? I couldn't tell.

"Merida!" Mum came into the kitchen. "Where have you been? I've been worried sick!"

For a moment, I felt happy. "You were?" Had the spell worked already?

"I didn't know where you had gone, or for how long. I didn't know what to think!" Mum sighed. "But you're home now, so that's the end of it. I've pacified the lords . . . for now. Your father is entertaining them."

My smile faded. The lords were still there. Nothing had changed. I held out my cake. "It's a peace offering," I said. "I made it. For you!"

Mum looked delighted. She picked up the fork and popped a piece of cake into her mouth.

"Interesting . . . flavor." I could tell she was trying not to make a face.

I wondered how quickly the charm would take effect.

"How do you feel?" I asked. "Different?"

But Mum didn't know what I was talking about. She took my arm. "Now, why don't we go upstairs to the lords and put this whole kerfuffle to rest, hmm?"

Nothing happened! I tried to hide my disappointment.

We neared the Great Hall. I could hear my father singing his song about Mor'du.

Just as we entered the room, Mum stumbled a bit, and I caught her. "I'm woozy suddenly," she said. "My head is spinning like a top."

I was getting the feeling that maybe that strange Witch's charm was working after all!

"H-how do you feel about the marriage now?" I asked.

Mum looked confused. "Just take me to my room."

We struggled through the Great Hall, where my father was attacking an enormous old stuffed bear as part of the entertainment.

The lords hurried over when they saw us. They demanded a decision from Mum about the marriage, but she told them she was ill. She looked pale and green. When she let out a burp that set the whole castle to quaking, I knew something was wrong. I hauled her off to her room.

She groaned as I helped her into her bed. "What was in that cake?"

"Cake?" I laughed as if I didn't know what she was talking about.

Mum moaned and wrapped herself in her blankets. With a thud, she rolled off the bed.

"So I'll just tell them the wedding is off, then," I added hopefully. I went around to the other side of the bed.

Something was going on beneath the covers. A form was taking shape, but it didn't look like Mum. The bedsheet writhed, then rose higher and higher.

Then the sheet fell away, revealing . . . a bear!

The bear growled and lumbered toward me.

"Bear!" I screamed.

The bear turned. It saw its own shadow on the wall behind it and scooted toward me. It threw its arm across me, as if to protect me.

I screamed, and the bear looked down at its paw. It grabbed a mirror. With a roar of surprise, it rose, hitting its head against the

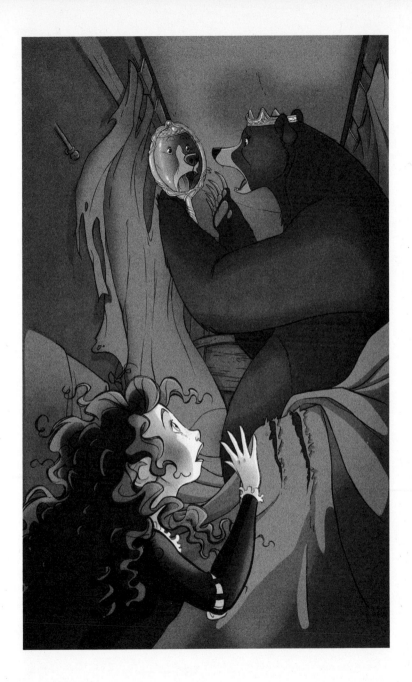

ceiling. It tripped over the bed and smashed a chair to pieces.

There was something very strange about this bear. Something oddly familiar — and, I realized, something horrible.

"Mum?" I asked.

The bear stared at me.

"You're . . . you're a bear?" I couldn't believe it. "That scaffy witch gave me a gammy spell!"

Mum roared loudly enough to rattle the castle stones.

I knew we had to get out of there—quickly. My father the Bear King would track Mum in no time!

Mum stumbled out into the hall. She was graceless on her short bear legs, knocking things off the walls. We heard people coming—it was

Dad and the lords, looking for the bear they had just heard! "Quick," I said to Mum. "This way!"

In her confusion, Mum ran the wrong way. I tracked her down in Dad's Trophy Room, where the walls were covered with the heads of bears he had hunted. But Mum wasn't looking at the bear heads—she was looking at my brothers. They were taking heads off the walls, and Mum was scolding them.

Of course, Mum couldn't speak. She could only growl like a bear. The funny thing was, those boys knew their mum, bear or not, and they did exactly what she told them.

When I walked in, my brothers stared at me.

"A witch turned Mum into a bear!" I explained as we ran into the hall. "We've got to get out of the castle! I need your help."

I couldn't have asked for a better team. The triplets created a phantom bear by holding a roasted chicken in front of a torch. Its shadow looked just like a bear! The triplets used the shadow to lure Dad and the lords away from Mum. The men followed the shadow "bear" all the way to the roof of the castle. Then the triplets locked them out!

Next, my brothers frightened the maids from the kitchen so Mum and I were free to make our escape. I grabbed a bow and headed for the door. But Mum hesitated. She didn't want to leave the boys.

"They'll be fine," I told her. "You've got to hurry." I managed to push her out the door. "I'll be back soon," I told my brothers. "Go on and help yourself to anything you want, as a reward."

Then I hurried off after Mum.

I took Mum to the Ring of Stones. I looked for the will o' the wisps to lead us to the Witch's cottage. Naturally, now that my mum was with me, they'd disappeared. "I was standing right here and the wisp appeared right there!" I told Mum. "Then a whole trail of them led me off into the forest."

I pointed, and Mum set off into the woods. I could tell that even though she'd never admit it, she had no idea where we were going. That didn't stop her from leading the way.

It never did.

Finally, we arrived someplace familiar. "Mum!" I cried. "I know this place! The Witch's cottage is close!" I ran toward it, and Mum followed right behind me.

Filled with hope, I opened the cottage

door—but the Witch was gone! Then I saw her cauldron. It was boiling and steaming. As I stared, I saw the image of the Witch's face in the steam above the pot.

The face in the cloudy vision seemed to be speaking as it nodded toward a clutter of vials. "If you'd like to inquire about a pre-order, pour vial one into the cauldron. For store hours and shipping rates, vial two. If you're that red-haired lass, vial three."

That message was for me! Quickly I reached for the third vial and emptied it into the cauldron. The potion hissed and boiled in the great pot. Then the Witch in the vision spoke again.

"Ah, the red-haired lass! I forgot to tell you: At the end of the second sunrise, the spell will be permanent unless you remember these words."

I listened carefully to the voice coming from the cauldron. It was a clue! "Fate be changed, look inside, mend the bond torn by pride."

I heard the clue, but what did it mean? There was just one thing I knew for sure: that Mum would be a bear forever if I could not find a way to undo the spell in two days' time. Frantic, I began looking for a way to get more clues to unravel the Witch's riddle.

I grabbed some potions and threw them into the cauldron. *Instead of getting a better clue to change Mum back into herself*, I thought, *I got a hot cauldron.* But before I knew it, the old pot seemed to overflow. Steam poured out, and I was suddenly standing in a thick white fog. I couldn't see a thing!

Then the white mist lifted. I began to see shapes around me. They were shapes from the cottage—but everything had been destroyed. The cottage was in ruins. The Witch's misty face was gone.

Mum and I looked at each other, then at the rubble all around.

There was nothing to help us.

ᘒᓍᘒᓍ

We spent the night in the ruins. I woke to the sound of clinking dishes. Mum had found something to use as a table. She had also found a couple of chipped plates and placed forked twigs as utensils at the settings. Even as a bear, Mum was a proper queen.

Then she started to eat a few berries she had put on the plates. I must say, she was quite dainty about it—for an enormous bear.

There was only one problem. "They're

nightshade berries. They're poisonous!" I said.

Mum spat out the berries. She filled her cup with water from a nearby jar and took a swig.

I looked into the jar. "Where did you get this water? It has worms in it."

Mum spit out the water and glared at me.

I slung my bow over my shoulder. "Come on!"

Down at the river, I shot a fish with an arrow. Bears love fish.

But Mum made a face as I held it out to her.

"How do you know you don't like it unless you try it?" I asked. She waved me off.

I cooked the fish for her. She devoured it and asked for two more. Kind daughter that I was, I caught two more fish for her and cooked them. Then she wanted even more—a lot more! I told her to catch them herself.

Mum had no idea how to catch a fish! I had

to get on all fours and show her how to catch one in her mouth. After that, Mum was much better. She caught one. Then another. Then we started to work together, both of us catching fish. It was the most fun I'd had with Mum in ages.

Suddenly, without a glance at me, Mum ambled off, walking on all fours.

"Hey, where are you going?" I called.

Mum didn't look back. I raced and caught up with her. I touched her and she turned. But I could tell by the sudden cold blackness in her eyes that she didn't recognize me. She sniffed me, just like a real bear would do. Then she raised her paw. I thought she was going to swipe at me.

Mum snapped out of it. She shook her head and stood up. Her eyes grew warm.

Mum was back. But that moment had made

me nervous. It was as if—for a second—she had become a bear on the inside, too.

Just then, a blue light flashed nearby. "A wisp!" I cried.

Mum dove after it, trying to catch it in her claws. "Just calm down," I told her. "Listen."

We were silent. Sure enough, the whispers grew until the forest echoed with them. Then I saw the trail of wisps leading us deeper into the woods. "They'll show us the way."

We followed the wisps through a thick mist to a decaying gate. A pair of crossed axes was carved in stone at the entrance. I had seen that symbol before, but I couldn't remember where.

Mum and I made our way toward the ruin beyond the gate. It looked like an ancient castle that had sunk into the frost-covered ground. I had no idea why the wisps had brought us here.

To the side of us was a loch. As we looked,

a large, scaly tail slipped into the murky water. Shuddering, I stepped forward—and fell straight through the ground, landing in a dark room that was eerily quiet.

Light filtered into the hole above. I saw that the room was a shambles, covered in frost and overgrown with roots.

Mum poked her head into the hole. She grumbled at me with worry.

"I'm fine, Mum," I told her, brushing myself off. When I stood up, I noticed four crumbling thrones. "You suppose this could have been the kingdom in that story you were telling me?" I asked Mum. "The one with the princes?"

I spied a large stone tablet. Figures had been carved into it. They looked like princes. Remembering Mum's tale, I counted them: "One . . . two . . . three . . ." The fourth prince had been split off from the rest by a crack in the stone. He held two axes across his chest, but his face was scratched out with claw marks.

In fact, the whole room seemed to be covered in claw marks. They seemed to be the markings of a very large and very strong bear!

Suddenly, I remembered where I had seen the crossed axes before. On the Witch's ring—the one she'd said the prince had given her! I was standing in that prince's throne room.

"Split," I murmured. "Just like our tapestry." As I ran my fingers over the crack in the tablet, I had a flash, like a vision. I saw the prince raise his axe and cut the stone in two, splitting himself off from his family.

A chill ran down my spine as I recalled the Witch's story about the prince who had visited her and was changed forever. The spell—it had happened before! I'd wanted a spell like the

one the Witch had given the prince. But I was starting to think I had hoped for the wrong thing.

The prince had wanted the strength of ten men, and he'd gotten it. He'd become a bear—forever!

Unless I could break the spell, the same thing would happen to Mum.

I looked around the dank room. That was when I noticed that even the stone columns were covered in claw marks. Bones littered the floor. I knew of only one monster big enough to cause such destruction: Mor'du. I'd stumbled right into his lair!

At that moment, I heard raspy breathing behind me. When I turned, I saw two eyes gleaming in the darkness. Mor'du.

Mum roared as I shot an arrow at him.

The arrow hit his shoulder, but Mor'du barely seemed to notice. I shot again, but it was no use. I jumped away, scrambling over a pile of bones.

Mor'du leaped out of the darkness, swiping at me with terrible claws.

I climbed onto a fallen beam and reached toward the ceiling. Mum pulled me up and out of the ancient room. A moment later, Mor'du's head burst from the hole.

Mum spied a crumbling stone wall. She tipped it over, collapsing it over the hole. It would only trap him for a moment. But that was long enough.

I jumped onto Mum's back. She tore full-speed through the fog. I watched over my shoulder as the ruin faded into the distance behind us.

I'd just met the bear that had taken my

father's leg. And now I knew what my mother's fate would be if I didn't set things right.

The Ring of Stones suddenly rose out of the mist in front of us. Mum scrambled to a stop just before we crashed into one of the stones.

"Mum, we have to get back to the castle," I told her. "I won't let our story end like Mor'du's. I know what to do. It's the tapestry!"

I had to repair it quickly. If I understood the Witch's riddle at all, then I had to mend the bond torn by pride—and I had to do it before sunrise!

**W**e made it back to the castle as fast as we could. While the guards patrolled the castle wall, Mum and I sneaked down to the moat. We sloshed our way through the water and climbed up the well into the courtyard. Once the guards had passed, we went into the castle through the kitchen.

The hallways were dark and deserted. "Where is everybody?" I asked.

Just then, we heard shouts coming from the Great Hall. When Mum and I peeked inside, we saw the men from the clans ducking behind overturned tables. They were firing arrows and throwing axes and anything else they could find at each other. All four clans were locked in battle. It was just as Mum had predicted—the clans were at war because of me!

"You've got to stop them!" I said to Mum.

But Mum was still a bear. There was no way she could enter that hall.

I had to do it.

I made my way through the fighting, straight to the center of the room. The arrows ceased and the war cries faded. Everyone stared at me.

"What are ye doin', lass?" my father asked.

"It's all right, Dad," I said, lifting my chin. I tried to look the way Mum did when she delivered a speech or ordered me about. "I—I have been in conference with the queen."

The lords started bellowing. They demanded to see my mother. They wanted to know how they could be sure this wasn't a trick.

"We'll not stand for any more of this jiggery-pokery!" Lord Macintosh cried.

The clans let out war cries. I only had a moment before things got out of control again.

"Shut it!" I hollered at the top of my lungs.

They shut it.

I saw Mum across the room. She was standing against the wall, pretending to be a stuffed bear. No one had noticed her. I took a deep breath and began. "Once, there was an ancient kingdom, its name long forgotten."

"What is this?" Lord MacGuffin demanded.

I ignored him. "That kingdom fell into war,

and chaos, and ruin," I told them.

"Och, we've all heard that tale!" Lord Macintosh sneered.

"Aye, but it's true!" I insisted. "I know now how one selfish act can turn the fate of a kingdom."

Lord Dingwall scoffed. "Bah! It's just a legend."

"Legends are lessons. They ring with truths," I responded.

Mum was still pretending to be a stuffed bear. But I thought I saw her face soften at my words.

"Our kingdom is young," I went on. "Our stories are not yet legends, but in them our bond was struck. Our clans were once enemies. But when we were threatened from the sea, you joined together to defend our lands. You fought for each other. You risked everything for each other."

The lords straightened themselves proudly.

"My dad rallied your forces, and you made him your king. It was an alliance forged in bravery and friendship, and it lives to this day." The clans cheered. "But I've been selfish," I continued. "And there is the matter of my betrothal. I've decided to do what's right and . . . and . . ."

Across the room, my mum shook her head. *No*, she was saying. *No*.

My heart leaped. Mum mimed breaking something. What was she saying?

"That we might dare to . . . break tradition?" I guessed.

The lords looked at one another. Mum put her paw over her heart. She was telling me what to say. I translated as best I could. "My mother . . . the queen . . . feels in her heart . . . that we be free to"—I interpreted more of my mother's mimes—"write our own story. Follow our hearts. And find love, in our own time."

My own heart was full to bursting. All I wanted was to go give Mum a hug. But I couldn't draw attention to her.

Even the lords were choked up. "That's beautiful," Lord Dingwall said with a sniffle.

"What can we say?" Lord Macintosh grumbled. He was frowning. "This is—"

"A grand idea!" Young Macintosh cried. "Give us a say in choosing our own fate."

"Aye," Wee Dingwall added. "Why shouldn't we choose?"

The lords gaped in surprise. Lord MacGuffin

turned to his son. "You feel the same way?"

Young MacGuffin muttered something that sounded like "yes."

"That settles it!" Lord MacGuffin cried. "Let these lads try to win her heart before they win her hand . . . if they can!"

Dad put a hand on my shoulder. "Just like your mum," he said, chuckling.

"Everyone to the cellar!" I shouted. "Let's crack open the king's private reserves to celebrate!"

The only thing Scotsmen like more than fighting is celebrating. With a mighty cheer, the crowd hurried out of the Great Hall and down to the cellar.

Finally, Mum and I were alone. We had to get to the tapestry.

Upstairs, in the Tapestry Room, I tried to pull the tapestry off the wall, but it wouldn't budge. "Mum! I could do with a wee bit of your help," I said.

But when I turned, I saw Mum sniffing a cabinet. Then she came closer and sniffed me. Her eyes were black again—like those of a wild bear.

"Not now!" I begged.

At that moment, the door burst open. Dad stood there, gaping at the bear. "What the—?" In a flash, he drew his sword.

"Dad, no!" I shouted loudly—desperately. "It's not what you think!"

"Merida, get back!"

Dad swiped, cutting Mum's arm.

"No! Dad—don't hurt her!" I screamed.

But the Bear King wasn't listening. He

swiped again. Mum roared and lashed out, knocking Dad to the ground.

Then her eyes cleared.

"Mum!" I cried. But we had been too loud. I heard the lords coming up the stairs, drawn by our shouts. "Mum, run!"

She nearly plowed over the lords as she raced from the castle.

"Dad!" I ran to help him to his feet.

"Are you hurt?" he cried.

"It's Mum!" I tried to explain. "It's your wife, Elinor!"

"You're talking nonsense!" Dad said. I tried to tell him about the Witch and the spell, but he wouldn't listen to me. He locked me in the Tapestry Room and gave the key to my brothers' nursemaid, Maudie.

Then my dad went out to hunt my mother.

I tried to break down the Tapestry Room door. I threw a chair at it. I tried to pry it open with a poker from the fireplace. But it was no use. It was a castle-grade door, and it wasn't budging.

I tried smashing the window with the poker. But it was only a narrow turret window, and there was no way I could squeeze through. I watched, helpless, as Dad and his men tracked Mum, the so-called "wild" bear!

"No!" I cried, slumping to the floor.

Just then, the tapestry caught my eye. I had

to sew it back together—before it was too late!

With a fierce yank, I pulled the tapestry off the wall. "Maudie!" I shouted. "I need you!"

I peered through the small window at the top of the door. Maudie stood there clutching the key. But she wouldn't unlock the door.

Suddenly, three little bear cubs appeared alongside Maudie . . . with crumbs on their faces. "Oh, no!" I groaned. I remembered telling my brothers to take whatever they wanted as a reward for helping Mum and me escape. They had eaten the rest of the spell cake. They had turned into bears, too!

Maudie took one look at them and ran away screaming, the key in her pocket.

"Get the key!" I told my brothers. I would worry about changing them back later—I had to save Mum first.

The triplets darted after Maudie while I searched the Tapestry Room for a needle and thread.

Thankfully, I found a chest packed with sewing supplies. Just as I was plunging the needle into the tapestry, I heard a bear cub howl. One of the triplets had climbed atop the others so that he could reach the window in the door. He held a key in his paw.

⁂

When I got out of the Tapestry Room, my brothers and I raced through the castle and out to the stables. We climbed onto Angus's back and galloped after Mum and Dad.

Angus knew the way. We were chasing Dad and the rest of the men from the clans. They had left a clear-enough trail to follow!

It was frightening. I knew they were chasing Mum. She must have been terrified. Dad's dogs were howling as they sniffed and tracked her. The men were shouting. It wouldn't take long for them to capture her.

I did my best to sew the tapestry while on the back of the bouncing horse. I wished I had paid more attention to Mum's sewing lessons.

"Done!" I cried, just as Angus reared and stopped. I took a look around us.

A blue light flickered before us. A will o' the wisp! A line of wisps lit a path into the woods. I urged Angus to follow them. "Hyah!"

As we reached the Ring of Stones, I saw that the lords had bound Mum with ropes. She roared with fear as my father raised his sword.

My arrow deflected the sword just in time.

"Get back!" I shouted at Dad. "That's my mother!"

Dismounting Angus, I stormed over to my parents, my brothers following behind me. "Mum, are you hurt?" I called.

Dad shoved me out of the way, and Lord Macintosh held me back. The Bear King raised his sword again. I flipped Macintosh over my shoulder and grabbed another hunter's sword. I used it to block my father's sword. Then I threw myself in front of Mum and, with a heavy blow, I chopped off my father's wooden leg! He fell to the ground.

"I'll not let you kill my mother," I told him.

My brothers, who were still bear cubs, ran up and held Dad down. I called them off. "Boys!"

At my order, the triplets ambled away.

Dad gaped. "Boys?" he said. A light shone

in his eyes, as if he finally believed me. But we weren't safe yet.

At that moment, Mor'du stepped into the Ring of Stones.

"Kill it!" Dad screamed as the evil bear reared to his full height. The lords' sons ran forward, but Mor'du swatted them away like pesky flies. He closed in on my father, who had staggered up off the ground on his single leg.

"I'll take you with me bare hands," Dad growled. But Mor'du grabbed Dad in his teeth and tossed him against one of the giant stones.

The demon bear turned to me. I nocked an arrow, but he ripped it away. He crouched over me. I was sure I was breathing my last.

Then I heard Mum roar. With new strength, she threw off the ropes and the men who held her down. She stepped forward to face Mor'du.

My heart was in my throat as the two huge bears grappled. Mor'du slashed Mum's face with his claws, but she fought back—hard. It was a frightening sight!

"Mum!" I screamed. Mor'du took Mum by the neck and tossed her against a stone, cracking it. Then he turned to me.

Mum reached for Mor'du again. As he charged her, Mum stepped away from the stone. Mor'du hit the towering rock with a mighty thud. An enormous slab of the giant stone teetered . . . and toppled.

Mum darted away just in time, and the giant slab fell on Mor'du, crushing him.

A blue wisp floated away from the stone. The ancient prince's soul had joined the other will o' the wisps.

I rushed over to Mum and watched in horror as her eyes turned cold and black. She was becoming a wild bear. I grabbed the tapestry and threw it over her.

Alas, nothing happened. I had nothing else to offer. Weeping, I buried my face deep in Mum's fur.

There was silence all around us as everyone watched in awe.

"I want you back, Mum," I said. "I . . . I love you," I said through tears.

I hardly noticed the dawn beginning to break. The sun was rising, its light crossing the ground toward us. This was the second sunrise that the Witch had given as a deadline. And Mum was still a bear!

Under the tapestry, I suddenly felt a hand stroking my hair. It was a human hand. My mother's hand. I looked up into my mother's face. She was smiling at me. She was no longer a bear—she was Elinor, the queen. My mum.

"Mum!" I cried as she laughed.

I loved my mum, no matter what. That was all it had taken to undo the spell and repair the bond we had. We hugged and laughed and cried. Mum covered my face with kisses.

I touched her cheek where Mor'du had clawed it. There wasn't a mark on her. "Mum, you're fine."

"Perfect," she said.

"Elinor!" Dad cried. He struggled up to his single foot, then tumbled, somersaulting toward us. Laughing, he pulled us into a hug.

The lords gathered around. "Welcome back, Your Majesty!" Lord Macintosh said.

Mum smiled, then looked down. That was when we both noticed the same thing. She had the tapestry around her, but . . .

"I'm naked as a wee baby," she whispered to Dad.

His mouth dropped open.

"Don't just stare at me," Mum said more urgently. "Do something!"

"Avert your eyes, lads!" Dad shouted to the lords. "Show some respect."

The men turned away. Just then, three red-headed little boys ran to us. My brothers were human again, too. And not one of them had a stitch on!

"Now, that's what I call a wee naked baby!" Dad roared. He picked up Hamish and tossed him into the air.

The sun had risen, and the light shone down on my overjoyed family.

The bond between us that had been torn was now fully mended.

⁂

From then on, peace reigned in the kingdom. Mum and I worked together on a new tapestry. It was an image of me with Mum as a bear. In it, we are facing each other, holding hands.

When the lords left, Mum, Dad, and I gathered to see them launch their boats. We waved as the boats pulled away.

Suddenly, Dad let out a grunt of surprise. At the top of each of the three ship masts was one wee redheaded rascal. My little brothers. Smiling, they waved to us as poor Dad jumped into a rowboat to retrieve them.

Peace reigned . . . most of the time.

The Witch was right—it is important to look inside ourselves when we disagree with the ones we love. I suppose I had to go the long way around to understand. But with that understanding came a bond between my mother and me that could never be broken.

As for the rest, eventually I married, and in time, I became the queen of DunBroch.

But that's another story.